Won't somebody play with Annabelle Kay?
She's all by herself on her very first day.

Her dress is so old!
Just look at her hat!

Now how could we play with a girl like that?

When Annabelle said that she wanted to play, the children all laughed and they sent her away.

Was there something to smile about?

No, not a thing.

She was there, all alone, by herself on a swing.

At home by her window she heard them outside, laughing and going on bicycle rides.

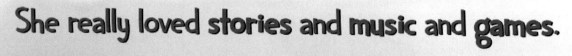

She really loved stories and music and games.

But when you're alone...   ...it just isn't the same.

Her flute made her happier when she was sad.

Music, it seemed, was the best friend she had.

"We know that you're lonely. We know that you're new...
But since you play music, that's what you should do!"

"There's a girl named Molly who's been feeling sick.

Do you think there's a way you could help her a bit?"

Annabelle frowned and she just shook her head.

If they won't be nice
Why should I be?

she said.

The sound that came out curled and swirled about. It danced through the air and it climbed up the stairs.

Annabelle smiled her biggest smile.

Her biggest smile
in quite a while!

It didn't take long for the word to get out!

The news that the city is talking about...

Twenty-one flutes are all playing today!

They're marching with Annabelle leading the way.